W9-CIQ-280

To Phoebe.
A.H. Benjamin

To Lumi.
Anne Vasko

On the Way Home
Somos8 Series

© Text: A.H. Benjamin, 2021
© Illustrations: Anne Vasko, 2021
© Edition: NubeOcho, 2021
www.nubeocho.com · hello@nubeocho.com

Text editing: Caroline Dookie, Rima Noureddine, Rebecca Packard

First Edition: May 2021
ISBN: 978-84-18133-22-0
Legal Deposit: M-16536-2020

Printed in Portugal.

ON THE WAY
HOME

A. H. Benjamin   Anne Vasko

nubeOCHO

On the way home **GRANDPA** said,

"We'll be just in time for dinner."

"I'm not **REALLY HUNGRY,** Grandpa."

"Well, we'll have to do something about that!"
he said.

So we did...

On the way home
we met a **MONKEY** swinging in a tree.
"Can we do that too?" we asked him.
"Of course!" said the monkey.

On the way home we met
an **ALLIGATOR** jumping in a puddle.
"Can we do that too?"
"Sure!" said the alligator.

On the way home we met
a tap dancing **ZEBRA**.
"Can we do that too?"
"Go ahead!" said the zebra.

So we did...

TA-TAP!

TA-TAP!

TA-TAP!

On the way home we met
a **TIGER** bouncing on a trampoline.

"Can we do that too?"

"Climb on!" said the tiger.

BOING!

BOING!

So we did...

BOING!

On the way home we met
a **HIPPO** lifting weights.

"Can we do that too?"

"Have a go!" said the hippo.

HUMPH!

OOOGH!

So we did...

AAAGH!

On the way home Grandpa said,
"Are you hungry yet?"
"I'm **VERY HUNGRY,** Grandpa!"

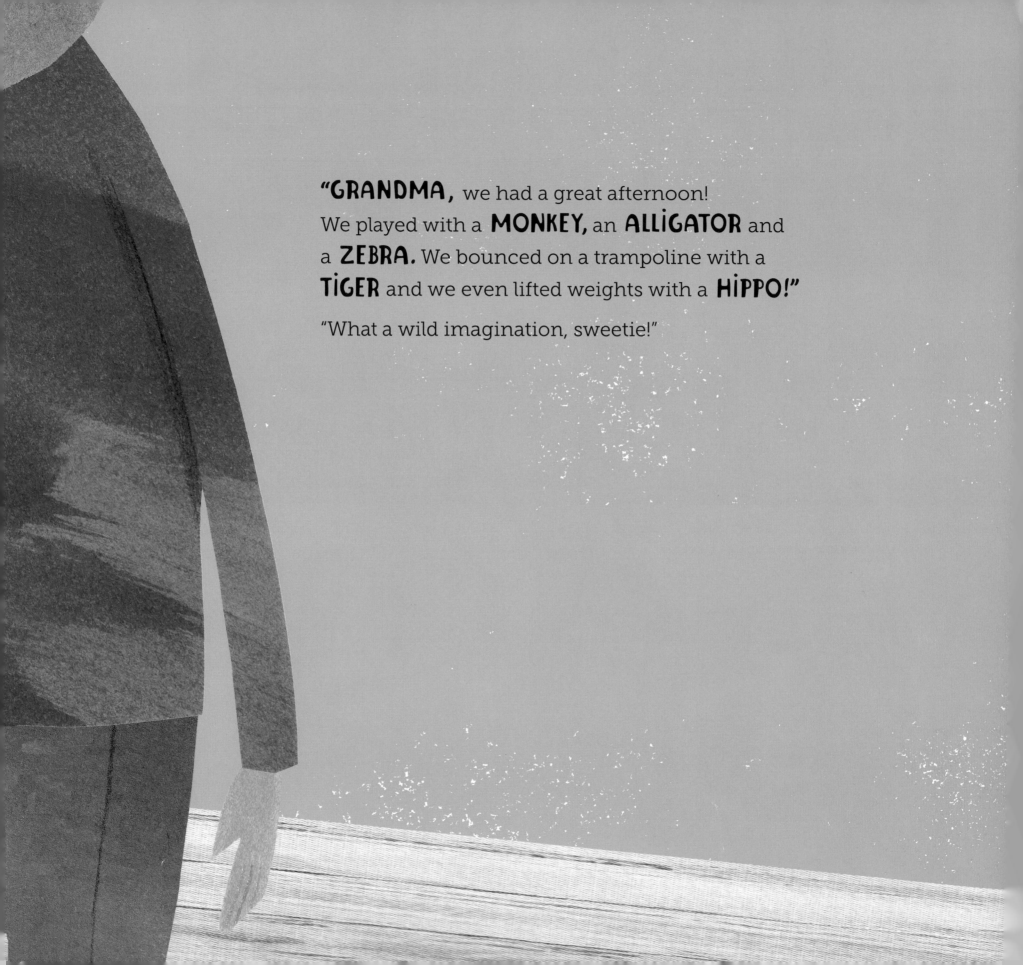

"**GRANDMA,** we had a great afternoon!
We played with a **MONKEY,** an **ALLIGATOR** and
a **ZEBRA.** We bounced on a trampoline with a
TIGER and we even lifted weights with a **HIPPO!**"

"What a wild imagination, sweetie!"

KNOCK!

KNOCK!

KNOCK!

"Who can it be?" Grandma said as I opened the door.

The **MONKEY,** the **ALLiGATOR,** the **TiGER,** the **ZEBRA** and the **HiPPO** were there!

"Surprise! Can we have **DiNNER** with you?"

"Yes, of course! Please come in!" I said.

AND SO THEY ALL DID!